THE REAL PLACE OF WOMEN

A QUEST FOR WOMANHOOD

MD NAUSHAD

Dedicated to every woman in the world who does the job of handling relationships, for which they do not get Mehtana.

Contents

CHAPTER ONE

HIGH HEELS

Those were the days of Delhi's Aerocity, when I saw the world of high heels for the first time from such close quarters. Where he worked, there would be a gathering of people of status. The smell of fresh coffee and beer mingled in the beautiful evenings. Long debates on the country and the world. That place was full of expensive suits and ties. There, expensive blouses and silk skirts rustled. And of course - all the time the heels resonated.

From blue-violet to glass-transparent, or even animal print, these heels were actually power-heels. Just like a tie for men. Then one day I met a woman whose veins in her legs were swollen and swollen. There was pain in the back and the doctor even said that if you wear heels for a long time, permanent damage can also happen. She was sobbing while telling this in the ladies room. Tapping my hands, I gave two or four Indian explanations. The next morning the woman was again in high heels. Eyes as if saying that the pain may be there, but by taking off the heels, I will not become a 'lesser woman'.

A study on this came out this month in the journal Personality and Individual Differences. In the study titled 'High Heels and the Perceived Attractiveness', a total of 448 men were interviewed. Everyone believed that wearing heels made a woman's body look sexier, more youthful, healthier and more of a 'high house'. Such a woman is a Kashmiri apple, which everyone wants in hand.

It was in the year 2013, when the famous French shoe designer Christian Louboutin was giving an interview in his apartment in

Paris. The interviewer questioned the high-heeled sandals and Christian said in a soft voice – when women wear heels, their body shape improves. The pace slows down. This gives the men a chance to see them. Christian went on to add that what is the point of running when a man calmly wants to see them! A woman running has always been seen as a threat. She will go fast and go ahead. There will be an attack, she will run away. Will be able to give a great presentation with straight legs in the board room. The flag can be hoisted by climbing the highest mountain. This is more dangerous than turning the earth upside down! So to control the running women, heels were tied on the lines of fetters on their ankles. Now they will run at the same speed which is pleasing to the men.

If understood in the indigenous way, then this is a game of spoon-pill, in which the woman who handles the marble in a shallow spoon leaves everything else, except being a woman! Yes, men find a lot of shame in this. In the year 2018, Murdoch University of Australia wanted to understand what kind of footwear men like women in.

Study results men blow away the mind. They absolutely reject cracked slippers with thick bottoms. A woman walking in such slippers, kept in a sack of potatoes, is a stale potato, which has rotted and which can be thrown away immediately to keep the rest fresh. On the other hand, the women wearing heels are the icing adorned on the cake, which can be seen from across the glass, even after seeing the eyes.

In high heels, the back part of the body takes the shape of a curve. The captivatingly taut body signals that the wearer is 'ready'. to meet. Actually this position is called lumbar lordosis, in which the spine appears in a particular shape. In all mammals, this position of the female tells her sexual sensitivity. So when the same rule applies to other animals, why should women get concessions!

So those who refused to do so were punished. British actress and journalist Nicola Thorpe was wearing slippers when she reached the office in the winter of 2017. Even before she reached her chair, the news of this matter reached her boss. At first he was asked to come wearing heels in a soft tone, but when he refused outright, he was sent home. Nicola, who had traveled about 25 kilometers from home to office, was returned because she was not wearing heels.

The talk would have been over if she had reached high heels the next morning, but women have a habit of prolonging the talk! Five months later, he launched a campaign against his company and appealed to the court that no company can make such extravagant demands from its women employees.

It was a different kind of #MeToo. Millions of working women started telling their stories. Started telling that companies not only take work from them, but also look like decorated dolls. Some were punished for not wearing heels, some for coming with natural lips. Many European companies want their female employees to touch up on makeup every hour. Well, let's talk about Nicola, after a lot of negotiation, it was finally settled that the company will not force you on makeup or heels, but if you do, you will get a little higher position than other fatiharin women.

The story of Cinderella was written in Italy in the 17th century. From then on all the countries started making their own Cinderellas. These stories would have been of a beautiful girl, glass shoes and a prince arrested in love. The circumstances made Cinderella a princess by her shoes and makeup. So even the fairytale women are being made to be Cinderella's younger sisters. However, now this illusion of fakeness is breaking down. Many women, including Nicola, are refusing to find a prince at the cost of jewelry and rags.

CHAPTER TWO

PERIOD

Recently, a picture came from the French Open in Paris, in which the female players are blindfolded and some people are handling them. This 19-year-old tennis player is Zheng Qinwen, who said after the defeat - I wish I was a man, I would not have periods, nor would I lose. According to Zheng, it was her first day of periods, when she had to play with convulsive nerves and abdominal pain.

Quite a simple thing. That truth, through which almost all women pass month after month, but this thing seemed like a challenge to the masculine mind. They win the battle after suffering so many deep wounds and don't even do it - here a young girl is pretending to be in pain.

People started saying on social media – nowadays girls throw tantrums of pain. Somebody started writing – If there is so much trouble, then why did I go out to play, sit at home! Somebody started writing – Our mothers never made such excuses about cooking or washing clothes.

That's right! Girls lick the pain and are doing it continuously. When Mian Pyaar returns to the office after tidying up, instead of a cup of tea, he finds a scattered house. The kitchen is filled with the smell of old chopped onions. On one side stands a small mountain of unwashed clothes, on the other side, a group of children are woven together, blowing their noses. Here the wife is sleeping adjacent to the door of the room. Reason? She has had periods. When the husband cooks the food, then she will wake up.

This tantrum will last for a day or two and will continue till menopause does not come. After this the sound of crackling of bones will resonate. The men of the past were wise, they knew that once women were allowed to cry, they would go on expanding like the stomach of a rich man.

That's why he stopped even searching for pain medicine. From the year 1590 to the next one year, there was a search for such women in Scotland who used to treat pain. Who would find such herbs in the forests, which can pull the pain. Or she would cook broth in the kitchen, which would give strength to the woman.

It is believed that such women are witches, who are making the world hell by removing pain from the lives of women. In fact, pain was a way of keeping blunt women busy, whether it was in childbirth, or by beating. Pain was that whip, which prevented the women from running erratically and kept them entangled in the household.

In the same period, Euphem Mac-Calgene, a woman from Edinburgh, claimed to have created a pain reliever during delivery. The women of the flock started arriving to ask for medicine. That was enough. Euphem was caught and thrown into the fire. The sound of his scream was drowned in the burst of fire. After that there was silence for many years. No woman has sought or searched for medicine to reduce pain.

By the end of the 19th century, anesthesia ie sedation drugs came. However, the women had nothing to do with it. It would be useful to men, who returned after losing or winning a battle, who were injured in a fight with a neighbor, or who had some other problem. The use of anesthesia was prohibited on the woman who was screaming in pain and dying during the delivery. A woman who cannot even give birth to a child with her hard work, how will she handle the rest!

This is the 21st century, but the situation is still no different. According to a 2019 report by the National Library of Medicine, hospitals still differentiate between genitourinary and masculine pain. If a woman comes to the emergency room complaining of pain, she is made to wait for a long time, while taking the complaint of men seriously, treatment is started almost immediately. That is, the pain of women is not urgent, but can wait.

In the year 2018, a case in France was in discussion, in which a 22-year-old woman, Naomi Musenga, called the emergency with a complaint of headache. Sobbing, she said - there is so much pain that I can die! The doctor posted in the emergency replied in a philosophical tone – one day or the other, everyone dies! After waiting for five hours, when the service finally reached the woman, she had died of stroke and organ failure. On asking for an answer, the doctor posted in the emergency said with a sighing throat - women often make small things big. So could not pay attention to the matter! If a woman complains of a headache, she will cry at night. If you talk about chest pain, then you must have eaten spicy. If you tell pain in the stomach, then there will be some sporadic disease of sure women. If you complain of pain in your feet, then you are getting old. Doctors give anti-anxiety medicines to most of the women who crowd the hospital with such minor complaints.

A study in 'The New England Journal of Medicine' suggests that women who come to the hospital with complaints of pain are often prescribed medication for mental illness or stress reduction, while men are fully screened.

Queen Victoria was the first woman who sought medicine to reduce pain during labor. The doctor treating the queen agreed after much debate that he would give her a little bit of chloroform, just so that she would not die. This is about April 1853. The Queen was also relieved as much as she could live. There was no talk of ending pain then, nor does it happen now.

CHAPTER THREE

WOMEN DRIVERS

It was the year 1910, when many parts of the world were reeling from the Industrial Revolution. New things came in that era, in which cars were also one. Now variety of cars started appearing in the market, but who buys! Then it happened that companies started dropping prices to cover the cost. This method worked. People who got the shoe made from Chuttan's shop and told him Oxford-Made also reached the showroom by queuing up. Everyone wants their own chic car. The face of the streets began to change. Long and short motor cars replaced the pedestrians. The people who slept till late, woke up looking, wearing their coat-tie and started going on a walk. Evenings were reserved for car-travel with family. All was going well, but before the car could get the first scratches, World War II broke out. Young and middle-aged men started leaving young wives in the trust of jealous old neighbours. The question was - what will happen to the car now! There was also a chance - also Dastur. Hands making soft bread and crunchy dumplings took over the steering of the car. Hesitating at first. Then with reckless trust. Children were dropped from school, greens and vegetables were brought, then there came a time when women who were burning in the distance from their husbands also started taking out cars to entertain themselves. Somebody goes to the coffee house. Somebody explored the forts and caves. At the same time, some people started driving to see the setting sun in the descending evening. Flying, this news reached the husbands fighting the war. That's where the mess started.

The husbands who returned from the war dusted off their uniforms, then grabbed the car keys first. Alfaaz very soft- 'You handled everything for so many days. rest now. Race has made you manly! Go, put some cucumber on the eyes, cream on the lips.

With sweaty hands, the wives handed over their newly-minted freedom along with the keys to their husbands. The jokes made on the 'woman driving the car' made up the rest. Mention of these manly jokes is found in the book Women drivers!: The emergence of folklore. Writer Michael L. Berger uncovers one by one how the secretly but meticulously plotted to remove women from the driving seat.

Even Russia, infamous for poisoning and killing its enemies in new ways, may not even weave as sure a net as it did to take the steering from the hands of women. Poison was not given. The fight didn't happen. There was no insult. Just made jokes.

If women are driving, then the accident is certain. She can put round roti, bake fun cakes, but can't park a car. To test a woman's endurance, leave her with the car in traffic. Give your wife all the freedom, just keep the car keys with you...! Endless letters. These poison-quenched Latifs very secretly snatched the freedom that came from the women.

The women themselves began to believe that they did not drive as luxurious a car as their mother-in-law, or brother or father. They started sweating in the name of parking. Seeing the crowd started panicking. In this way she slid from the driving seat and came to the side. He no longer had 'his' car. She will travel only when her man wants. Anyway, the kitchen ring is pleasant in the hands of the janana, not the key of the car or bike. The Taliban understands this very well, only then a decree came out from the Driving Institute not to issue licenses to women. This news came from Herat city of Afghanistan two-four days ago. There is no direct ban on women driving on the roads, but there has been a ban on issuing new driving licenses.

Gradually, the number of girl drivers will disappear from the roads. Let us tell you, this is the same city of Herat, where a few months ago an order was issued to remove the Janana Mannequin from the shops. According to the Ministry of Propagation of Virtue and Prevention of Evil, live men can be deceived by seeing effigies of women with measured bodies in shops.

This game of delusion is not limited to Afghanistan, for a few years a new trend has started in airplanes, which started in the year 2015. The flights coming from New York to Israel suddenly started arriving late. When the reason was searched, it was found that some male passengers were averse to sitting next to unknown female passengers. Belonging to a particular community, these men felt that sitting with a female traveler would disturb their chastity. They started demanding that they would remain in their place, but the women should be picked up and sent to another seat. Failure to do so created a ruckus and flights got delayed.

There's even a video for men called the Spiritual Safety Video. In this it was told in which ways the female co-traveller should be kept under control, that her knees should not touch, or her hair should not fly on her face. There was a demand for full body safety vests so that men could maintain their purity by entering that shell.

Later, some rebel women started an online campaign against Israel Airlines, after which there was little change. Now on the Israel-America air route, no man demands that a female hitchhiker be removed from his side or else he will become unclean. No body wears vest. Nor does it shrink its nose and eyebrows by looking at women, although that much change is not enough.

The real change will come when women can be as comfortable on the road as they are at home. Or else- change will come when men can be as comfortable seeing women driving cars on the road as they are.

CHAPTER FOUR

WOMEN AND GAMES

The seventies were about to end, when the US state of Connecticut was hit by a storm. The reason was girls. 19 girls of Yale University were sitting on dharna. She was half naked. On the open part above the waist, he had written 'Title IX' in blue letters.

This is a change related to education, which opposes the difference between men and women in sports. On a bright day, devotees gathered to see this protest on the chest and back. Pictures started being taken. Saliva remarks started pouring in on open bodies. The girls still stood still.

The war finally paid off. The university recognized that girls also sweat. They also hit the ground when they fall. Dust settles on them too. They also have wounds. So in this way lockers and showers were arranged for female athletes.

Doctors were kept in the dressing room. Heaters were installed so that on snowy days the female players did not die by murmuring. All these arrangements were in place for the male players from years ago, but the girls had to undress for this.

This American anecdote of the seventies becomes more ugly after reaching India. Recently a book came out - Not Just a Nightwatchman. In this book of IAS officer Vinod Rai, there are many sensational revelations about the game. Vinod Rai explains that there was no separate uniform for women cricketers, but only clothes made for men would have been trimmed and worn by women. According to Rai, he called the company making jersey and said sternly that this would not work. After this, women could get their own separate uniform, which was according to their body.

Well, sports is not the work of women either. Due to this, the ups and downs of their bodies are no longer interesting enough for men to get lost in. The body becomes masculine. Hands become hard. Chest flattens. Even the face loses its softness. Only the beard and mustache are left behind.

Now how can such a woman feel good? Men want wives who are beautiful like dolls, whose skin is covered with diamonds and the body is as soft as cotton.

So women were kept away from all kinds of races. Even by horse riding. To ride a horse, both legs would have to be put side by side, there was a danger of showing the knees of the woman wearing the skirt. This danger was greater than the collision of a fierce inverted body on the earth.

This too was broken. It was announced that the wombs of mounted women slide down. Then she can never become a mother, that is, no longer a woman. Now the girls who were fond of sitting on the horse were left with only two ways. Either they sit behind the husband holding his waist, or they should run the horse with both feet on one side.

Yes, with both feet on one side! Imagine a woman riding a bike or a bicycle with both feet to one side. At what angle should he keep turning his neck in an attempt to see the road? How far can she walk! How many more or less accidents will happen! How many pain medicines will he have to take after getting off the horse?

The conspiracy was successful. The women themselves gave up on horse riding. After many moons, around the year 1930, he could get the freedom to run a horse by spreading his legs. This was a period of war, when men were needed for everything from running the house to spying. In this way, due to the masculine need, some freedom came on the part of the women.

Let's leave other sports and come to swimming. Swimming is the exercise in which 50 muscles of the body work at a time. This is fine for men, but this quality can be dangerous in the case of women. If the muscles become active, then women will become stronger than the body along with the heart and mind. Then she will not answer the slap by shedding a tusk, but with a slap. So swimming was refused to be considered 'lady-like'.

Stories were made that by being fascinated by virgin girls, the devil of the sea subdues them and takes away their virginity. Even after this, when the women did not agree, a special dress was designed for them. These would be robe-like gowns, which were heavy from below so that they would not rise up in the water. There would be dark colors, such as black or blue, so that the body could not be seen even when wet.

Bathing machine again! It was like a small house with wheels at the bottom. They were lowered deep into the sea with the help of horses and machines so that the women could also fulfill their hobby of playing and jumping in the water and the purity would also be maintained.

The times changed The women of today have the 'exemption' to have a physical appearance. However, this change, resembling freedom, turned out to be the beginning of slavery. Women's clothing became increasingly smaller, and tighter. At the same time, the clothes of the male players were such that they could breathe.

During the Olympics last year, Germany's women's gymnast team chose comfortable clothes instead of short clothes. Men speechless at this! Hey, we came to see his bare arms and fleshy legs, not to watch the game.

After this, the Norwegian women's handball team also wore shorts instead of bikini bottoms. Eventually, the European Handball Federation furiously fined him thousands of pounds.

The masculine anger at women players wearing long dresses is justified. After all, the women who entered the playground are a kind of charity. If you return after playing, you have to run a ladle, take care of the crying children, caress the angry husband.

In 2006, tennis player Venus Williams wrote a letter through The Times of London, in which there was a line - 'I am a second class champion! With me the rest of the women's champions too. First class is for men'. Soon after Williams' letter, women and men started getting equal amounts for winnings in tennis.

16 years have passed since that letter. Now awaits the new Williams, whose letter can take another step towards parity.

CHAPTER FIVE

SECOND EARNER

It was autumn in America, when the beautiful Khawatines (women) working at Google stopped their long fingers gazing at the keyboard, and rebelled against the company. He said that despite equal work, he gets less salary than his male colleagues. They were three women, while against whom he made a statement, he was one of the selected most powerful companies in the world.

The company kept in denial, but the women kept on sabotaging it like a drunken elephant. After all, after five years, Google admitted that there has been a 'little-lot' of ups and downs. In return, he will now pay more than $118 million in compensation to 15,000 women, including the women suing. He is happy In such a cheap way, for the next many years, he got an unfair exemption from crores of working women of the world.

The 16th century was passing, when women started going out of the house for work. She worked in retail. Like preparing fresh bread every morning, picking seasonal fruits, cleaning the house, or grooming the clothes and hair of a wealthy housewife. If enough, feed his children and teach him the piano. These women worked month after month, year after year, but looked to their husbands even for sporadic needs.

The reason was that the salary received at the beginning or end of every month would go to his husband. This was the English law, which was immediately copied by the slave countries. So in this way there were millions of such women around the world, who used to work without money.

In fact, they used to be husband's property then. Just like a piece of land, or horses and goats. All of them had only one job, to make men richer, and happier. Wives also fall in this category. So just as sheep and goats could not make their own property, in the same way women also had no question of property, whether they sit at home or work throughout their life.

Women are 'secondary earners' anyway. That is, those who earn more money than their partner. It's not us, it's the search engines. As soon as you put these words on Google, many articles go on opening, where women are being talked about in a soft-hot tone. She works for Timepass. With her own money, she buys perfumes, chooses clothes, and brings gifts for the family. At the same time, his salary falls like two-four drops on a hot pan and disappears from the filter.

In the year 2018, the Gender Gap Report of the World Economic Forum came out. India ranked 108th in this study conducted in a total of 149 countries. That is, even for the same work here, men get more money, women get less money. No matter how educated you are, no matter how hardworking you are, if you fill in the female column in the gender column, you will fall short. Being a woman is your first disqualification.

The story does not end here. A study by Hive shows that women work 10 percent more hard than their male colleagues in the office. Not because they don't work, or because they learn late. Rather because in addition to the fixed tasks, non-promotable tasks are also given to them. The work, which she cannot write in the resume like a tag, nor does she get a promotion in return.

For example, taking a newly arrived colleague to the coffee machine, explaining office rules, helping a sick colleague, or comforting a stressed team. They are also responsible for making Rangoli on Diwali-Holi and making a list of sweets.

Apart from all these 'non-essential' tasks, the daftaria also handles the tasks. Also does research and makes presentations. The picture is reversed as soon as you enter the board room. She is able to present the same presentation sitting quietly on the chair to a man who remained 'Miyan missing' the whole time.

The Netherlands, which stands first among the countries giving equal rights, recently did a study. The study, titled 'Parental Leave Reform and Long-Run Earnings...', sought to understand why women lag behind in terms of salaries. Its results are astonishing. According to this, in spite of paid leave, the father is afraid to take leave on the birth of the child so that upon returning, his prestige in the office may not decrease.

The situation is even worse in Australia, where the mother's name is included in the primary care-giver section, meaning that men can leave crying babies and weak mothers and go to the office comfortably. This condition is more or less in every profession, and in every part of the land. According to the World Economic Forum, the year 2277 is the time when women and men will get equal pay for equal work. More than two hundred and fifty years. That too, when no other corona comes in the world, or there is no war.

CHAPTER SIX

Controversial Deodorant Ad

It was at the end of the Second World War, when soldiers were returning to their homes in ships. Here the women wrapped in the smell of vegetables and meat were engaged in shining the house. It was an attempt that their husbands who came back should forget the fatigue of the war. Then came an advertisement, the first line of which was - 'Beautiful but stupid!' Obviously, it was talking about the wives.

Perfume maker company Odor-o-no has ads - women do not know the first law to look beautiful. She takes care of her face and hair, but remains suffocating with sweat. In such a situation, the man who comes close also gets separated from him. The more this smell of sweat increases, the more romance will run away from the woman's life!

By the year 1946, there was a flood of advertisements from perfume-full to keep the inner parts of the woman as pearly as pearls. Now, if we talk about this add-on of perfume, the company's profit has increased manifold within a year. After this, every woman would sweat, but the fragrance of lotus would have mixed in it. Even after sitting in the kitchen for hours, that ocean of fragrances would hurl from the wife, that the husband would have forgotten everything in a hurry.

Now after about 75 years, a new add-on of perfume has come. For boys! But wait, this doesn't have to be a trick to seduce girls, but just a hint of gang-rape. This perfume advertisement named Shot starts with a couple. They are in the room when the door opens and four boys come in. The couple gets spooked. One of the boys says- Shot seems to be hit! The boy sitting with the girl says- 'Yes'! This time he has a look of masculinity on his face.

Resting his hands comfortably on the bed, he is giving a green signal to the rest to 'shoot'. Fear and astonishment mingle on the girl's face, when one of the four walks forward and picks up the perfume bottle from the table, almost drowning her in fear. There is relief on the girl's face to pass by the rape.

In the masculine world, the tradition of taking sarcasm on rape is very old. American comedian Reginald D Hunter said during his show - If there was no rape, then civilization would not have progressed! The whole auditorium shook with laughter before Hunter finished speaking. The comedian repeated this recipe of laughter in many meetings after this. If there was no rape, then civilization would not have progressed!

Australian comedian Jim Jefferies was known for his rap-comedy. In a show filled with a lot of laughter, he told – I liked a girl. He refused to be in bed with me....(after a long silence) So I raped him. It was a joke, on which the audience started laughing and rolling at each other.

Why only advertisements, the whole world of art is adorned with naked women or women shedding tears in blood. Pablo Picasso, famous for his skills all over the world, made a picture, which was named - Weeping Woman, that is, a crying woman. The painting was by French artist Dora Mar, who was Picasso's girlfriend at that time.

It was said about Dora that she would have been a better artist than Picasso, 'if' worked, but she could only love. In this way, she became a crying girlfriend and ended in loneliness. For many years later, Picasso used to decorate his ex-girlfriend's picture at exhibitions.

Women are not allowed to be artists. With a big heart, she started becoming an inspiration to the artists. More or less every painter or photographer or writer would have got such a wonderful girlfriend whose eyes are deeper than the Nile. Which is as fresh as the morning dew, and whose color is as if sprinkled a pinch of vermilion in butter. The bulges of the body should be more attractive than any maze.

In the early nineties, an American feminist organization spoke of this male dissociation in art for the first time. Guerrilla Girls reported that only 5% of the artists in the Modern Art section are women, but about 85% of the artwork included here is by nude women. That is, all male artists are painting their canvas with naked and full-bodied women.

There was a slight uproar at the revelations and it disappeared just like the sound of a flute in a fish market. Even the movement of Guerrilla Girls into art galleries was banned so that they do not create any disturbance there.

CHAPTER SEVEN

Attention hungry

First they killed my husband. Then the two boys. After that they started dragging me and my 10-year-old girl. Laughing they were saying – we do not kill women and girls, we only rape them. When we reached the road, we saw that there were shackles looking like handcuffs everywhere. Our clothes were torn and our hands and feet were tied. Now we were part of the road - ready to be trampled under every foot.

'How many soldiers, how many men raped me, I do not remember. Whenever I fainted, buckets of water were thrown at me. As soon as he regained consciousness, the process of rape would continue. One day I found out that my daughter was dead. I want to die too.

When Mukuninwa, who had lost both her intestines and eyes in the rape, said this in the International Criminal Court, there was no silence in the room, there was no sound of anyone crying and crying, but a question came like a punch on the chest – you have so much Why didn't you raise your voice for years? Many judges also wondered how the women were able to survive in spite of so much barbarity! This is after the Great African War. Let us tell you that a few years before this, in the year 1998, the ICC had given the status of rape to 'also' war arising out of war, but giving status is a different thing, being sensitive is another.

One of the well-educated and justice-loving judges argued - When an injury occurs, there is an instant scream. She doesn't wait for any particular time. If 'rape' is also a kind of injury, why don't the victims of the injury immediately cry? If a man abuses you, why do you keep silent for years?

The question was weighty. The less educated and the women who were crying after tearing the bookcase did not have the answer. This question arose about 20 years ago, perhaps even two thousand years ago, and will remain so even after two hundred years. At least that's what's going on here for the time being.

A few days ago, an award-winning male writer was accused of sexual misconduct by a chubby girl. According to the girl, the litterateur kept tyrannizing her for 10 years by pretending to be love. Now he is married and is shying away from her.

When a very anonymous girl disclosed this, she must have been hoping for justice. It may have been a naive belief that people will reprimand the man. But the opposite happened. The girl was asked why she remained silent for so many years! Or, in 10 years, could he not understand the difference between love and rape! The alleged litterateur did not need to say anything in his favor. The girl's not crying immediately put her in the dock.

When a little ladybug pricks its teeth when it falls on its feet, then the girls have gone through the ladybug worm too! Why do women who walk around with the flag of rebellion in their hands hide their faces forcibly! Many surveys have been done to understand this.

One such survey was published in the Journal of Occupational Health Psychology. The report, titled Raging Voice, Risking Retaliation..., said that if a female employee makes a complaint of sexual abuse against a male boss or co-worker, it is very possible that she may not get a job in any other company. People consider him to be a troublemaker and avoid hiring him. In the survey conducted on a total of 1,167 women employees in the US, more than 72 percent said this.

Most of them admitted that after complaining, other colleagues also avoid talking to them and even after being expert in their work, they remain like a tomato without a throat in a vegetable. It will give taste, but the eater will slide it on the side of the plate.

Sometimes the exploiter is the superstar of the company. Someone who gives a lot of benefits to the office. In such a situation, along with the car, the driver and the luxurious house, the company also gives him a discount so that he can entertain a little bit of junior women.

In the year 1621, Xu Yujiao, the ruler of the Ming Empire of China, scattered 5000 soldiers across the country for a specific purpose. The soldiers roamed around and started catching beautiful girls of 13 to 16 years. In the palace, he would have to be trimmed on many layers. Even the color of the skin in the sun and shade and the smell of breath after waking up would be checked, after which the true girl was sent to the king.

She was called concubine, whose job was to produce many children for the king. It was believed that beautiful and healthy girls have only one use - to produce children for the ruler.

During these 9 months the girls had to remain locked in the palace. There was a ban on going in the open air so that the demonic force swinging here and there should not capture the child. It was forbidden to bathe, wash the hair so that the child growing in the womb should not be seen anywhere. The pregnant would be made to sit in one place like a dough ball. So it used to happen that by the passage of nine months, a young woman with an agile body would become as unformed and useless as an old potato.

However, this is not a big price in return for giving strong children to the king. In return, she would get the job of a maidservant in the palace itself.

What are women to do anyway! Just have a little laugh. You have to say yes to the boss. And if he wants to come closer by speaking baby-shabby, then instead of getting angry, he has to talk about two or four juicy things. That's the only thing, but on this they weepingly reach Human Resources. Goes to court many times. That's why companies started distancing themselves from troublemaker women.

Sexual abuse is the only crime in the world where instead of the perpetrator, the perpetrator of the crime is punished. Some call him a mischievous, some greedy. 'Attention hungry' is also a term that sticks to the foreheads of girls when it comes to sexual abuse. Now the girls are speaking though. Some years later, some immediately.

CHAPTER EIGHT

The Real Place Of Women

There is a happy news for women that science has found a way to measure their beauty. Deep eyes, pointed nose and delicate juicy lips even more than rose petals - how many fingers distance should be between them that the food should be called the most beautiful, all these secrets are revealed by male scientists. Meanwhile, another news came, which is not so fancy. According to this, the place of women in science is the same as in the class of a child who has failed for years. That is, they are nowhere.

Research done at New York University came in the well-known science magazine Nature Today. It shows that women working equally in science are also 59% behind men. They will work, but in 59 percent of the cases, the credit will go to Mardani's pocket. For this, 9 thousand 778 research teams from around the world were talked to, in which about one and a half lakh women and men were involved.

The male scientists themselves believed, if the names of women are known on any discovery, then people will not believe it. It is like, if the petty company claims to make the world's strongest slippers, then no one will believe. On the other hand, if a big brand is stamped on that slipper, then people will take it immediately. So people should have faith in science, good hearted men, that is why they remove the genitive tag from it and stick their name.

Women scientists go to the lab. Also touch test tube and computer. Stay awake all night and work. But when the discovery is announced, he stands in the corner to watch the male scientist carrying a bouquet with loving eyes. If you ever get upset, take out your lips and cry a little bit. Or go on vacation wearing a silk gown. Or start spinning the spinning wheel. Know for sure, the wandering of the mind will calm down from the morning. Anyway, whoever does the work, the real thing is that it should reach the common people.

Rosalind Elsie Franklin, born in London in July 1920, introduced herself as such. Rosalind is the scientist who discovered the structure of DNA. First of all! Working in the lab of King's College, his fellow scientist Morris Wilkins shared its picture among friends in anger. Morris acknowledged this in his memoir 'The Third Man of the Double Helix'. They were angry that Rosie was self-reliant and hardworking 'over-necessarily'.

At the very end, Rosie came to know that her search was not only stolen, but also divided like gram and murrah. She was on vacation. In the year 1962, the three men who stole pictures and shared among themselves received the Nobel Prize for the discovery of the DNA code. Rosie was in depression - as is the habit of the mothers. He left King's College. Eventually she died of ovarian cancer.

Who discovered DNA - Search it in Hindi or English - Rosalind's name will not be found anywhere. After winning the Nobel and Rosie's death, her fellow scientist Morris finally revealed that Rosie should have been credited for the original discovery of the DNA code. Morris had won the Nobel - he became great by speaking the truth.

The real place of women is in the kitchen, where they can experiment freely. If you want, add a splash of wine to the raskheer, or cook the brinjal with jaggery - their wish. Even if the taste of husband gets spoiled due to this, water will not come in the world. Lab is a different thing. Even a small mistake here can wreak havoc. Thus the habit of women to cry and sing!

This is the reason why the English biochemist Tim Hunt, who won the Nobel Prize, talked about removing women from science completely. In June 2015, he made a statement that instead of working, they (women) fall in love and when you point out their mistake, they shed tears. Then forget Khoj-Voj and keep wiping their tears.

In a conference between senior women scientists and journalists, Tim said – I am not criticizing 'girls', but either they should stay away from science, or separate labs should be made for them and us. Only then can something new happen in the world. There was a ruckus on the statement, but like a soft-drink bubble, it also calmed down. One more thing - when Tim Rondu was talking about the girls - the male journalists who came to the conference were laughing and rolling at each other.

So! Tim Hunt, the discoverer of the protein molecule, did not apologize to Rondu and the female scientists who fell in love. On the contrary, laughing and said – I have got the Nobel. He told what he experienced.

The reason is clear, how out of more than 600 Nobel Prizes received in science, the share of women could not reach even 50. Agents of Jananis create lakhs of gossip, with every search, the name of Johny will be etched by scraping the name of Jane. After all, it's a matter of trust!

CHAPTER NINE

VIRGINITY

It was the London of the 19th century, when rich men from all over Europe, including England, began to take their wives to the 'London Surgical Home for Women'. Here every genital disease was treated - not with medicine, but with a special surgery. In this, a sick woman would be circumcised, whether she had brain disease, cancer or seasonal fever. The treatment for not sleeping, or not digesting food was to cut the outer part of the female sex organs.

The name of the founder of the hospital was Dr Isaac Brown, who was a famous gynecologist of that era. They believed that the root of all the troubles of women was their sexual desires fluttering in the air. For them, circumcision is as effective as whipping a spoiled horse. They will come under control immediately. In his book 'On the Curability of Certain Forms of Insanity', Dr. Brown mentioned dozens of diseases that could be cured by circumcision. In medical parlance, this surgery is called clitorectomy. Thousands of men who returned home after getting treatment for their wives started writing long letters to Dr. They rejoiced at how his magical cure turned his woman into a maniac, epileptic or hysterical, rolling, lazy or ugly looking like a goat with a straight and silky face.

Nearly a decade later, the Royal College of Surgeons put a rein on Dr. Brown's one medicine trick for every merge. Not because he objected to this method of treatment, but because the doctor had not taken a hospital licence. Although the practice of circumcision on women is still going on. Earlier it used to be in hospitals, now it is happening in homes in the name of tradition. It is called Female

Genital Mutilation (FGM) in modern language. It is believed that this will protect women from many diseases. At the same time, her sexual desires will also be under control till marriage, so that she will be able to give the precious gift of virginity to her husband.

In 2022, girls of African countries stood up against this practice. Quoting science and data, she started telling how many girls died of pain and how many infections during this process in a few years. It is a different matter that his arguments remained as a returning voice echoing in the empty house. They are being beaten up, and if this doesn't work, they are being thrown out of the house. The insistence is that girls should remain clean by getting circumcised in any way.

Countries that did not believe in bloodshed like circumcision, they had another method of purity control. In this, the lower part of the woman's body would be imprisoned with iron. It would have been like lingerie with a lock on it. The man of the house would go out and put a lock on it and open it when he returned at night.

It was the chestity belt, that is, the best to maintain purity. Just like if a milk pan is kept open, there is a fear of insects, insects, dust and soil getting into it, in the same way, if a woman is not a firm guard of the body, then there is a fear of her going astray. This fear was relieved after the discovery of the chest belt. Suspicious husband would go to work after putting a lock on his wife.

It is another matter that many times wives would have died due to some infection, but what is better than death while being pure!

In later years, many museums of the world decorated their chestity belts. In the caption below, there is a complete description of how the whims of men have committed atrocities on women. As was expected, soon there was opposition to this. The men feared that this would make women lose their trust in him. Then what was there! Instantly all traces of the chest belt were erased. The British Museum in London finally removed it from display in 1996. Now hardly any trace of it can be found in any museum.

The trend of chestity belts has gone, but the craze of purity regarding women still remains. In November 2019, famous

American rapper Clifford Joseph Harris (TI) revealed during a podcast that he gets his daughter's version test done every year. Talking as a father on the 'Ladies Like Us' podcast, Harris says – My daughter turned 18, but I am proud that she is still holy!

Harris is not proud that his daughter is a noble person. Not even if she is studying well, or will be able to do better in future. A father is proud of his virgin daughter. His only achievement is the purity of the body. He may or may not become anything else, but he remains pure. Or continue to give the illusion of purity.

CHAPTER TEN

COSMETIC SURGERY

It was the beginning of the nineties, when Princess Diana spoke about her illness for the first time. Diana, with transparent blue eyes, admitted - I would feel hungry, but I was afraid of even an inch of fat on my waist or arms. With puffy cheeks, I used to fear the same thing as someone with cancer. I was afraid that Charles might leave me.

Fear made me sick. Sitting at the royal table at Buckingham Palace, I ate food, but went to the bathroom to put my finger in my mouth to spit it out. I wanted to disappear - like a drug that dissolves when you put it in water.

One of the most beautiful princesses in the world, Diana was a victim of a disease called bulimia nervosa. She was afraid of obesity, just like a child would be scared of snatching her most beautiful toy. Slender and glass-transparent body is the only wealth with women, the only weapon to live in the masculine world. In handling this capital, Diana made herself ill.

In 1993, with tearful eyes, he admitted that his condition was like that of a sheep, which is in captivity, and is just waiting to be bitten. The needle of time moved forward 30 years, but the fear of women about obesity remained there.

This fear of women about invisible obesity is not new. In the early 17th century, European women wore corsets. This would have been a special dress, which would have made the top and bottom sections very embossed while keeping the waist at 18 inches. In order for the woman to look attractive, girls were put in corsets from an early age.

Just as people who are fond of trees decorate banyan in the bedroom by making bonsai, on the same lines the body of women also started getting bonsai. They began to be cut and cut. Even if the woman's body does not spread like a fool after getting the exemption of pregnancy, for this also such a dress was made, which could control all the other parts of the body except the stomach.

In this effort to keep the body attractive, women started losing their lives. The science journal Lancet studied corsets every year continuously from 1860 to 1890. It was revealed in this that only one cloth is doing as much harm to women as no deadly disease can do. A total of 97 diseases were attributed to this, ranging from 'minor' problems like indigestion of food and trouble in breathing to internal bleeding.

People with protruding stomach, while taking pictures, hold their breath many times and do the trick of pulling the stomach in. These Victorian women were under pressure to stay on their stomachs round the clock. Simply because they were women. They were not allowed to earn arm strength. Bookish skills were also not his part. If she searched the world while sitting in a ship, she would have been killed. After leaving one body, it became his weapon, skill and wealth.

There was no surgery for weight loss then. The only solution was to trot like a chiraya and wear stifling clothes. In addition to the corset, a variety of iron structures were created, filling the woman with a haphazard body into which, after filling, a lowly Kamini came out. For years, generous men spent all their creativity on making women's clothes.

In the year 1850, a special skirt came, which was called crinoline. It would have been tight from the waist and bloated like a balloon at the bottom. The skirt would have had an iron frame under it, which would have prevented it from sticking to the legs.

After wearing it in silk above and iron cage below, women could neither board the bus nor in the horse carriage. She could only walk a little, lifting her feet lightly. Accidents also happen many times because of the ghoomardar enclosure. However, this cost of looking beautiful was far less than what could be seen by men. Over time men became more liberal. Now they do not ask their women to eat less or wear stifling clothes, but instead point their little fingers towards surgery.

According to data from the International Society of Aesthetic Plastic Surgery, in 2019, 86.5 percent of all plastic surgeries performed worldwide were performed by women. She is trimming fat, making breasts more voluminous, wanting a sculpted nose and making lips more juicy than strawberries.

Well, now they are free to do everything. If she wants to roam, no one will stop her way, just assuming that she is a vagabond, she will rape her. If you study more, you will be called stale pearls. If you want to become an artist, you will face the agreement.

If you only want to take care of the house, you will be called a fool. Not getting rid of it even after that. After death, such women go straight to hell, who, with their ugliness, stir the hearts of hardworking men.

Nowadays a more modern, more sophisticated way of grooming women has come out. According to a study published in the American journal 'Research in Social Stratification and Mobility', companies pay better salaries and posts to women who have thick lipstick on their lips and foreign perfume is magnified by expensive clothes.

It is a conspiracy that the woman should spend her whole life in grooming. This is what is happening. The 21-year-old actress dies while fighting an invisible obesity. Millions of women suffer severe pain every year while shedding fat. It would have been better if instead of the body, they could get rid of the haze on their minds. There would have been a surgery in which the woman who came out of the operating theater would have been everything – except the body.

CHAPTER ELEVEN

HUMOR GAP

It was in the year 1872, when Charles Darwin saw chimpanzees laughing at each other. Other scientists also observed this laughter and claimed that male chimpanzees tickle the females to attract them. That is, in the role of the male laughing, while the female laughing at his jokes. The study on chimpanzees has been applied to humans as well, but with a bit of confusion.

International Joke Day was celebrated on 1 July. There was a lot of talk about the claim that funny jokes not only make the day wonderful, but such a person also gets promotion in the job quickly.

The boss keeps such an employee with him in the presentation. The coolies stand in queue to go to tea with him. Even the guards standing at the door give a strong salute to such people, but all this only when the joker is a man. As a woman, everything takes a U-turn.

To understand this, the University of Arizona's social research team conducted a study in two parts, in which a total of 216 people were involved. The same trend was found in both private and government offices regarding joking people. Everywhere the funny woman was seen as a work evader and 'Available'. The women involved in the research also told that because of joking, the men started flirting with them. He was sure that telling jokes was also a kind of signal, which the shy ladies were giving in their own style. Research published in Applied Psychology called this difference the 'humor gap'.

Overall, the world of humor is that photograph, seeing the beautiful valleys, beautiful clouds and blue water, we go straight there after cutting the air ticket, but after reaching there is a different view. There is everything on the hills except mountains. Blue-deep water is as small as a pond. And, the noise is such that Kallu has come to Mian's wedding for a feast. The world of laughing and laughing has also become a similar illusion.

Most of the men's jokes in stand-up comedy revolve around the bodies of women. Some make fun of wife, some female boss. On the other hand, rape jokes are the cherry on the cake, which every man wants to keep in his mouth.

Of the 3,387 men in the Western Carolina University study, nearly 90 percent of men admitted to listening and reciting rap jokes in a jiffy. After such intelligence, they feel themselves more powerful. Many also believed that women are a thing to be ashamed of, whether they give at home, or in jokes.

American stand-up comedian Daniel Tosh became one of the country's famous comedians due to his rap jokes. A few years ago, when some feminist women protested against this, the answer was received - Now on this platform, if five men rape a crying woman, will it not be fun to see.

Tosh had to say that the male audience sitting below started whistling and started saying that feminists want to make jokes also a chapter of the school. They are as boring as their speeches. Then what was there! So many jokes have been made about the rape of women and their bluntness, that vegetables are not made from potato varieties.

Question-answer website Quora has a question - Why can't most women make jokes that make them laugh? Is it sexist to think of them like that? The question was asked by a poor, unnamed person. Well, without going into details let's read the answer - no woman is funny. Even if they try to tell jokes, they start laughing at the deception found in having children, meeting singers and dating.

Many women are able to joke about their obesity, or ugliness, but they do not even touch society, politics or such things. Now if such women start calling themselves comedians, then where will the poor men go!

Scientists from all over the world have written novels on how much jokes are liked by men and women. In a study published by the University of Kansas called Sexual Selection and Human in Courtship, it was told that if a woman laughs openly at the jokes of an unknown man, then it is very possible that she has started liking him.

This study was done on more than 2 thousand 5 hundred students of the university. It also showed that if the girl has more humour, then the boys run away from her. They are afraid that in future such a girl will overwhelm them.

How can men who are looking for a girl less than themselves in height, weight and age, how can they adopt a sharp girl. So the laughing girls are left alone until they give up and start laughing at the lewd manly jokes.

9 798887 497266

Printed by Libri Plureos GmbH in Hamburg,
Germany